Michael and Mr. B.

The Story of A Boy and The Bunny
Who Came to Teach Him Unconditional Love

Written and Illustrated
by Joyce Connor

"All Things are Possible!"

Joyce Connor

2007

Diamond Mountain University Press

Published in 2006 by

Diamond Mountain University Press
An imprint of Diamond Cutter Press
512 Newark Pompton Turnpike
Pompton Plains, NJ 07444

Website: www.diamondcutterpress.com

Interior and jacket design by Clare Cerullo

Printed in China through Colorcraft Ltd., Hong Kong

ISBN: 0-9765469-1-4

Dedicated with Love

to

GMR and Christie

James and Lisette

Liz, Ava Rose and Liam Connor

…and of course, Michael

With thanks to

Marilyn, Sonny and Everyone at Diamond Cutter Press

All proceeds from this book go toward the Global Wealth Initiative.

GWI is an international non-profit organization whose mission is empowering people through a compassionate worldview to create individual and global wealth.

Chapter One
The Questions

Up, up…I must get up! Something inside me said I needed to hop quickly from bed! I must have had a dream that made me think I should jump up this early on a Saturday instead of rolling back over into my warm covers…but I couldn't remember for sure. I was still groggy, but slid out of bed anyway. As usual, I made my way to the kitchen for a bowl of cereal. It was a clear November morning and the early sunrays were beginning to dance through Mom's lacy window curtains. I usually don't wake up so early on the weekends. But today was different for some strange reason…

As I was headed for the breakfast table, a thought stopped me first at the kitchen window. It faced our backyard and overlooked the garden where a few flowers were still in bloom. The day was just light enough to see the brightest petals remaining on some rose bushes. I yawned and rubbed my eyes to wipe away the sleep as I stood in front of the large windowpane.

Something caught my eye as I was stretching away the last winks of slumber. Was it the wind in the leaves? No, that didn't seem quite right. Something was creeping low to the ground! I looked closer. Could it be Nicky, the neighborhood cat, who at the age of 16 was still keeping the mice away? No, it wasn't Nicky's dark gray color. Perhaps, I thought for a second, it was that skinny white cat who comes to check the mouse hole behind the garden's rock wall. (We could never discover where this mysterious kitty came from, because we never saw her come or go. Every now and then she just appeared in our yard.) Looking closer, I realized it wasn't her either. That white cat was so-o-o thin and this creature seemed to be much more rounded. It certainly wasn't a wild turkey or any other bird we see scratching the ground to look for breakfast. What was it then?

I rubbed my eyes again to make sure I could see clearly. It only took a second longer to discover what it was! "Mom, Mom… please come quickly…look in the yard! Somebody's rabbit has escaped!" This wasn't an animal I'd ever seen before. Mom came to the window as I looked again to make sure I wasn't mistaken. We both wondered whose pet had run away.

Mom phoned our neighbors, Mr. and Mrs. Dennis, asking them to take a look. They gazed out their window, smiled and waved. All four of us were watching the area between our yards. Mrs. Dennis and Mom discussed whose pet it could possibly be. We all knew that some family had to be sadly missing their furry little friend! But who? Nobody we knew in the neighborhood had a rabbit. So where did he come from?

The bunny looked so awesome…beyond beautiful…black and white with long, lopping, velvety ears! He was a big spotted poof with a wiggly nose and whiskers. His eyes were glistening pink, like the color of a gemstone, with black fur patches around them. "Mom, look at the size of him… he's a *whopper hopper*," I said with a big grin. We decided he had to be the largest rabbit we've ever seen! He leaped back and forth between the two yards, acting quite at home. His soft fur stood out against the fallen brown leaves that lay around the rose bushes. What an unexpected sight to see!

I rushed back to my room and almost tripped on my long pajama legs after gobbling the fastest breakfast ever! I quickly threw on my old sweater and jeans. Scramble…scramble! Rushing faster, I barely got into both shoes before I ran to the back door.

"Michael, don't run toward him because that will scare him away," Mom cautioned. "He won't know you're friendly when he first sees you. So please go slowly." Even though I could never understand how Mom could be so calm in these kinds of situations, I tried to be patient. When I got to the kitchen door, I stopped running and took a deep breath. Maybe she was right. That rabbit didn't know me so I had to be careful. I was nearly silent as I walked outside and closed the door quietly behind me. It barely made a sound.

At first, the rabbit didn't react to seeing me. He was busy having a breakfast of the rose leaves that grew in our garden. I stepped as softly as possible up the stone path that ran beside the flowers. I was getting closer to this new ball of fur. But I was at least fifteen steps away from him when he caught me in the corner of his eye. He didn't hesitate for a moment, not even a second! He instantly cut to the right and high-tailed it back to our neighbors' yard! He jumped so high, it was like his feet grew wings…*a rocket rabbit*! He made tracks for some tall bushes and hid from sight. Gone in a flash!

I wondered what I'd done wrong? I was so careful in trying to get close to him. I had almost tiptoed in slow motion! I wasn't even a little bit noisy as I walked toward him. And it took every bit of patience in my body to go that slowly! But the rabbit still ran away.

I looked back over my shoulder at Mom. I must have had a very puzzled look on my face as if to say, "What made the rabbit run?" Mom smiled sweetly at me as she watched from the window.

Suddenly an idea popped into my head just like a light bulb turning on. CARROTS! If I am ever going to see that rabbit again, I'd better get some carrots from the fridge! The carrots were old ones and a bit limp. But I figured if he'd been on the loose for a while, he might not be too choosy. I placed a few in our neighbors' yard and some in ours…all in plain sight.

I went back inside the house, thinking it might take some time before his appetite returned. The morning was spent going to and from the window…watching and waiting. More waiting. Even more. But he was nowhere in sight. I thought he might be tempted to show himself in order to get a carrot. No such luck.

By afternoon, I'd almost forgotten there was a rabbit somewhere nearby. Then something told me to check the window again. "Yahoo!" I shouted and Mom rushed to the window. The carrot trick had worked! There he was…sitting in the grass, hungrily snacking on the treat I had left. He looked up at Mom and me with a face that said, "Thanks for the veggie…but *you* stay inside."

I could see it wasn't going to be easy, but I had a strong wish to pet his furry back! After all, it wasn't every day that a big black and white rabbit with ears that almost touched the ground came into my life. In fact, nothing like this had ever happened before. (Well, ok. There was that skinny white cat who magically showed up. She just didn't seem as exciting as a spotted rabbit.)

Mom suggested that I take the bunny some fresh food for his dinner if I really wanted him to be my friend. I didn't even have to think about it. "I DO! I DO want him to be my friend," I answered Mom right away.

"Then I have some ideas for you," Mom said as she walked toward the fridge. "A shiny new apple and some crisp lettuce leaves would be nice for the bunny. They're much fresher than the old carrots. Let's offer him healthy food that we ourselves would eat. Why don't we treat him as though he's already a member of our family?" Mom's suggestions made sense as usual.

I headed for the backyard again where the rabbit sat facing the field. I made my approach. I *softly* stepped closer. Once more, I got close enough to catch his sideways glance. Then *THUMPITY THUMP*, with two GIANT hops to the right, he jumped over the rock wall and was gone. PLOP… PLOP! Again, he had disappeared into the tall bushes. This rabbit was incredibly fast! There had to be some way to slow him down and let him know I'm friendly. But how?

I placed the red apple and leafy lettuce under a rose bush…offerings for a tasty bunny salad. I sadly realized that this fellow wasn't going to be an easy friend. By late afternoon, my hopes had been dashed not once, not twice, but three times. I decided to give it up for today and then look for him again in the morning. But when I wake up tomorrow, would the rabbit be gone?

He was still around the next day but continued his game of hide and seek. Mr. and Mrs. Dennis made phone calls and knocked on neighbors' doors, trying to find the bunny's home. Nobody knew of anybody who was missing a rabbit. We all agreed for sure, if he had been a caged critter who'd managed to break loose, he now had no intention of ever being trapped again. After several days of similar scampers as soon as I'd get close, I had to believe that our garden guest was determined to remain a free-range rabbit!

"How can I make him my friend, Mom? I don't want to hurt him, but he doesn't seem to know that." I let out a sigh of frustration. I needed her advice now.

"What you are doing for Mr. Bunny is so very sweet, Michael. Bringing food to the yard for him is such a thoughtful gift for a lonely, lost rabbit. I know he'll enjoy the treats." Mom gently hugged me as I looked up into her eyes. "But who knows? Maybe he didn't see such kindness at his last house. Perhaps that's why he broke free and went looking for a new home. I think it will take some time for him to trust you. It might not happen right away because his experience tells him that he doesn't want to be hurt. He's afraid and doesn't want to suffer. But if you're very patient and kind, and you're always that way with him, I think you'll see that he'll come around. Remember to just take it slowly. Perhaps he wants you to prove that you have only goodness for him." Mom always knows how to make me feel better.

I went outside and sat down on the garden path. As I looked out beyond the fence, I thought about how I might feel if I were that rabbit. Somehow I knew that what Mom told me was true. Why should he trust me right away? He didn't know me. If he came from a place where others weren't always good to him, how could he see me as his friend? I decided I would do as Mom said. I would just take it slowly and treat him with kindness. Then perhaps he would soon feel good about being my friend.

Two weeks passed since our first bunny sighting. We started calling him "Mr. B." and the name just seemed to stick. Every morning when I got up, I peaked out the window to the garden so that I could make sure he was ok. Each day the rabbit was there, either in the neighbors' garden or ours. A few times he was sitting in the field just beyond our yard. It seemed as though he was waiting to see if I would find him. It made me so happy to see him! Sometimes it felt as though my heart expanded just to lay eyes on him. For some reason, this bunny didn't seem like an ordinary rabbit.

Every night in my prayers, I asked questions about Mr. B. Where did he come from? It seemed that he wasn't from around this area. Nobody here had lost a pet. It was as if he'd magically appeared out of nowhere! Why did he stay? Why didn't he hop away? He didn't seem to want anything to do with me. So why didn't he move on to someone else's house? Was it because I left food for him? There were hundreds of rose bushes in the neighborhood that he could eat and yet he stayed here. I somehow knew that he wanted more than food from me. And I also thought he might have something he wanted to give. Could this be why we came into each other's life? I kept on hoping the answers would come.

Chapter Two
The Preparations

I had to make some preparations if Mr. B. was going to stay here. And it looked like he might. The November weather was quickly changing. Our sunny California skies were growing darker, and the winter rains would soon come. I felt that Mr. B. knew the warm, sunny days of autumn were coming to an end, because his spotted fur coat was getting thicker. He looked twice his normal size on cool mornings as he huddled down closer to the ground, then puffed himself up to keep off the chill. It seemed he might need some extra care.

One night it began to rain, rain, rain. The raindrops were as big and fat as any I had ever seen! It was still pouring when I went to the window the next morning to look for Mr. B. There he was… at the edge of the garden. I saw him pressed as tightly as possible against the rock wall. It was as though he was thinking that if he could make himself flat as a pancake, he could avoid getting wet. He couldn't. He was soaked to the bone. His spotted fur was clumped and dripping with water. Sometime during the night, he'd gotten tangled-up in a long bramble, which still clung to his matted coat. Mr. B. held his lopped ears as tightly as possible to his body in order to keep them warm. Rain was funneling down the middle of those long ears and pooled on the ground. Today he looked more like a drowned rabbit than a handsome hare! His face had a miserable expression as if to say, "Help me, Michael!" I knew then he had to have his own little shelter to give him comfort. The rains could last for months. Some years, it didn't stop raining until June. That was way too long for a rabbit to be wet!

We all agreed that this bunny was in need of a roof over his head. So Mom and Mrs. Dennis purchased a little rabbit hutch that would sit on the ground. The hutch was a rabbit house shaped like a small igloo, all rounded with a hole for his front door. We placed it behind the rose bushes, beside the rock wall, to protect it from the wind. I dropped rabbit food, like breadcrumbs, leading to the door. I bedded the hutch with straw for his warm mattress. It looked like a good place for him to nest out of the weather. The next day, and the next and the next, I took the time to take care of Mr. B. I hoped this attention would help him during the rainy season…and help him be my friend.

Ever so slowly, Mr. B. began checking-out his hutch. He'd eat every last food pellet right up to the door. He'd take tiny hops just to the opening and stick his head inside to check it out. It seemed he wanted to make sure it was safe. It was as though he was double-checking to make certain there were no other animals hiding in there! Then he'd back out again and head for a meal of rose leaves which he loved the most…more than carrots or apples or even the rabbit food pellets. Although the hutch seemed safe enough to me, Mr. B. was very slow to go inside and trust it for his shelter. He still hadn't made it his home.

The next night, I couldn't even fall asleep without first seeing that the rabbit had a good place to nest. "Is it alright if I look around outside, Mom? I'd like to take a few minutes to make sure Mr. B. is ok," I said as I looked out the window.

"Yes, my dear, you can check on him," Mom said. "But first, put on your jacket and please remember to be safe." She reached for the coat rack as I grabbed my blue baseball cap.

The night was black, so I stepped carefully. With flashlight in hand, I made my way to the hutch, hoping to find him inside. He wasn't there. I walked around the back yard in the dark, throwing the light beam ahead of me. "Where is he?" I asked myself out loud. I stopped and pointed the beam on the rose bushes, but there was no bunny. My head turned from side to side as I looked high and low through the garden. But I couldn't find Mr. B. anywhere nearby our house.

Startled by a noise, I looked up. "Hoo…hoo…hooooo!" A Great Horned Owl, particularly hooty that night, was perched on a low limb in the oak tree. He tipped me off and gave up the rabbit's hiding place. "Thank you for the clue," I whispered to the huge bird who was looking directly at the rabbit before looking down at me. I stepped through the garden gate to the neighbors' yard and threw the beam of the flashlight on a stack of firewood. A couple of pink eyes glowed back at me. Sure enough, Mr. B. had tucked himself away in a small space between two logs in their woodpile!

Although I was happy to have found him, I felt afraid for his safety. The woodpile was outside our fenced yard! There was just enough room between the iron bars of our fence for him to squeeze through. He could slip back and forth to come and go as he pleased. I knew it would be no time at all until some wild creature discovered his nesting place in the logs. The woodpile was not a safe place for him to sleep at night! I knew I had to try harder to get Mr. B. to understand he was in danger. I had to make him wise to sleeping in his hutch *inside* our fenced yard. I had to spend less time doing things for myself and take responsibility for him.

I became a man on a mission. I had to gain this bunny's trust…not just for selfish reasons…not just because I wanted a friend…but because he had to be saved. After all, there were wild animals out there looking for dinner. If they found him, they would make a meal out of him in a second! So many creatures passed through our neighborhood…coyotes, raccoons, and bobcats…even the occasional mountain lion. Mr. B. wouldn't want to tangle with any of them! I wanted to keep him safe. I had a job to do.

And if the wild animals didn't harm him, the bad weather might. Mom had spent some time studying about rabbits and learned that Mr. B. was the type that was not used to living in very cold weather. It was late in the year and freezing nighttime temperatures were headed our way. He needed protection. He was worth saving!

"I think he might be afraid of the hutch…scared that some hungry animal could trap him inside," Mom said with a worried expression. "Do you suppose we could make the hutch more bunny-friendly, Michael?"

"Maybe I could make a rear door, an escape hatch, just in case," I said. Mom thought that was a good idea, so I spent the next afternoon cutting out the rear door. Mr. B. watched me from a safe distance as he ate his favorite nectar of rose leaves.

The new door seemed exactly what he had in mind! I almost started clapping when he entered the hutch that very evening to take his rest! Mr. B. seemed to understand what I had done and that the hutch was going to make a good home for him after all. I aimed my flashlight from the kitchen door to see him in his new home. His sleepy face looked happy. I think I even saw him wink at me!

I began to think of Mr. B. more and more as time went on. I even had dreams about the two of us playing together. I had to figure out a way to get to know him so we could understand each other. But I was a boy and he was a bunny. Would I be able to make this happen? I still wanted to understand the mystery of where he came from, why he stayed, and figure it all out. That's when I decided to begin talking to him. Maybe…just maybe…he would see me as his friend after all.

"Mr. B…Mr. Bunny," I said softly as I made what seemed to be my 100th attempt at contact. "Why are you here? Where did you come from?" Mr. B. looked up from a snack and stopped chewing. His long ears perked-up high at the sound of my voice. His head tilted to one side then the other as he listened to what I said. He looked pleased that I was speaking to him. His sparkling eyes were the same color as the few remaining blooms on the Sea Pinks. And his mouth…I really thought I saw a little grin there! He seemed to be paying attention this time. But all too soon, he turned his back to me and went right on munching the leaves, pretending I just wasn't there.

Several more days passed. Each day, I tried a few more times to speak with him. I kept remembering what Mom said about him… "Take it slowly, try to be patient, and always be kind"…that sort of thing. So I did my best. I had more dreams that the bunny was my friend. And not only that, but he was just as important as any of my human friends. I dreamed his life was just as good, just as special, and just as meaningful as anybody else's. Each morning, I would awaken with these thoughts on my mind. I saw that they were true.

Step by step, I continued down the path of kindness. Day by day, Mr. B. let me get closer and closer to him. I always asked him the same questions. "Mr. B., why are you here? Where did you come from?" He would look up at me as though he understood what I wanted to know. I think he was beginning to see that I was there to help him be happy.

When I woke up the next Saturday, I had a feeling in the bottom of my belly that today was going to be different. But I had no idea *how* different it would be! As always, I started the morning outside with our big-eared, pink-eyed, not-so-friendly rabbit guest. As I crouched on the ground, stooping low, I got within an arm's length of him. My heart was beating faster and it seemed he might let me touch him this time! It seemed he might respond to my kindness at last. But hope is one thing and dreams coming true are another. I wasn't expecting the HUGE surprise that actually happened! I was about to discover that the questions I'd been asking him over and over hadn't been ignored. Mr. B. stretched his neck up high, wiggled his whiskers…*and answered me back*! Except his words weren't coming from his mouth…it was more like *his mind was speaking to me*! And he came through loud and clear. I could understand his words as though he were another person! *"WHOA!"* I know my jaw dropped open because I was so-o-o shocked!

I was shocked into understanding. Suddenly, I knew why I dreamed he was already my friend and why I should take good care of him. I then knew something for sure…the bunny had been speaking to me in my sleep! From that day on, Mr. B. began speaking to me while I was awake! For months, I wanted to hear from him and now that I was, I couldn't quite believe what I was hearing! Was it really happening? It seemed too good to be true!

"Michael," he seemed to whisper, "I *am* your friend. Excuse me for taking so long to tell you so. I wanted to teach you some things before I spoke. It seems to me that you've learned these lessons very well."

The bunny stood on his hind legs and looked right into my face with big wide eyes. He suddenly seemed twice as tall. His nose twitched and the words kept coming. "I wanted you to understand how important it is to treat each living being with kindness…the same kindness you would show yourself. *Each living being* means not only you humans, but all creatures, large and small. Every single one, from the little ones in your garden to the large ones in the forest, all need to be loved. You must be wise and careful to love the wild animals from a distance, never touching or feeding them. But know that they can feel your loving thoughts. They appreciate whatever you do to protect their forest home."

Mr. B. waited for these words to sink into my mind before adding the biggest truth of all. His bright eyes sparkled as he said, "Now, the incredible thing about what I'm saying is what you're going to hear next. So listen closely, because here it is… *Caring for others, giving them what you'd give yourself, doesn't just help them. The love you give them will all come back to you!*"

I was still surprised that I was listening to a rabbit speak to me! Trying my best to overcome my excitement, I concentrated all my attention on what he had to say. I found myself "thinking" right back to him.

"How is it," I thought, "that you can talk with me? And where, oh where did you come from?"

Mr. B. didn't hesitate. "Michael, you have special powers. Actually, we all have these powers deep within us, but some of us are able to call them up quicker than most when we need them. Do you know why you can do this? Do you know why this power to speak with me has come to you?" I'm sure my mouth gaped open even further as I realized I wasn't daydreaming.

"No, Mr. B., I haven't a clue why it is that I can talk with a rabbit…or how a rabbit can talk back to me! I mean, I feel pretty normal." As I said this, I pinched my arm to make sure I wasn't imagining it. I wasn't. It was really happening! I sat down beside Mr. B. to get closer. I wanted to hear more from him. He gave me a wise-bunny grin and hopped into my arms.

He began again, "You and I can speak like this from mind to mind because you already understand what I've been teaching you. You already know down deep inside that you must love every living being as you love yourself. Even when they make it difficult to be loved…especially then…you must continue to be kind. Keep giving goodness to them just as you would give it to yourself."

I relaxed and his words became clearer. "Michael, there were many days and nights you put my comfort before your own, even when I kept running away from you. You made sure I had a warm hutch for my nest and lots of food for my belly. Many times you put aside the things you'd been doing before I showed up, like playing ball or riding your bike, so that you could take better care of me. And remember how you went out each night with your flashlight to make sure I was ok? It was cold out here, but you came outdoors anyway to see that I was still cozy and safe in the home you made for me. You took the time to check that I was comfortable and made sure no coyote was near me. It's because you showed me such incredible love that I return it to you."

I thought about what he said to me. It made sense. It made me feel good that I could do these things for him and see to his happiness. And if I could do it for him, couldn't I do it for my family, my other friends and for all other creatures? Couldn't I do it for everyone? I felt strongly that I could. I decided that no matter what else I did in life, I would draw a circle of love around each living being and try to make life as good for them as it was for me. It was what I promised myself to do.

My talks with Mr. B. became a regular daily activity. We'd sit together in the garden on the few days when the weather was still warm and clear. He enjoyed taking short naps in my lap as I stroked his soft, furry back and ran my fingers down his black, velvety ears. He was at peace and so was I. We told each other we loved one another. He asked me to always treat each living being with the same love that we had together. I promised that I would.

Chapter Three
The Seeing

The heart of winter was coming soon to northern California. Mom and I began to discuss that the bunny hutch might not be warm enough for a rabbit like Mr. B. The wild jackrabbits who live in the woods behind our house were warmly burrowed in their bunny holes, dug into the ground. But Mr. B.'s home sat on top of the ground and was unprotected from the cold and rain. He wasn't a rabbit who would have wanted to live inside our house because he enjoyed his freedom too much. So we started to wonder how we could do more to help him get through the winter.

I covered the hutch with leaves and a blanket. But when it rained, the covering got soaked and made the hutch too cold. With two bunny doors, a front and back entrance, the wind howled and pushed the rain straight through. I often saw Mr. B. shivering inside the hutch that was supposed to protect him! And it wasn't only the weather that threatened his health. If he could hop in and out of the space between the bars in our fence, it meant that some other animals could get *inside* the fence, too. Was there a way to solve these problems? I tried very hard to make everything right for him. So why wasn't it all working better?

I wanted his life to be perfect! But I could see that the wanting wasn't enough to keep him safe. I found myself clinging to the idea that he would be ok if I just held onto him tightly. I wanted to believe that if I loved him enough, he would be able to stay with me and then everything would be right. But I couldn't seem to fix all the problems to protect a rabbit who wanted his freedom to live outdoors. So I said my prayers and waited for a solution to come our way.

One day, Mrs. Dennis came over to tell us that her cousin, Suzanne, was coming from Los Angeles for a visit. The winter months were much warmer where she lived and there was not as much rain. She said that Suzanne cared very much for animals and had kept other bunnies as pets. Then Mrs. Dennis suggested to me that Suzanne might like to help another rabbit.

Oh! My heart felt sadness at the thought of being without Mr. B.! He'd brought such joy and friendship into my life. It hurt to think of his living so far away. He was the bunny who talked to me in a way that helped me grow up. He taught me to take responsibility for others and think of ways I could make them happy. How could I let a friend like him go away? The answer to this question was simple…I wanted life to be good for him…as good as it was for me!

I imagined where Suzanne lived and it sounded like a wonderful place for a rabbit in winter… warm sunshine and blue skies. The more I thought about the home that Suzanne might give Mr. B., the more it seemed that he might be happier and healthier there with her. But I was still stuck on making that decision for him. Maybe I'd know the right thing to do if I saw how he felt about her. Perhaps Mr. B. himself would show me the answer I needed to know.

The Saturday came when Suzanne was to arrive for a visit. I got up at the crack of dawn and waited at the kitchen window to watch for her entry through the garden gate. I had to be sure that she was right for Mr. B., and he was right for her. I had to know that she'd love him as much as I did. I wanted to sense that she'd always do her best to look after his happiness. Most of all, I needed to know that he would feel good about her, too.

This rabbit had become such a sweet friend. It felt good to know I had done everything I could to make him happy. But it seemed that my work wasn't finished. Was there more I could do for Mr. B. and for some others, too?

As morning came into our garden, I saw Mr. B. standing on his tiptoes to reach some tender leaves high on a rose bush. They were always his favorite breakfast. I watched him with love in my heart and noticed how he only ate a few leaves. He always saved the flower blooms for Mom and me.

The sun was barely peeping over the treetops when Mrs. Dennis led Suzanne into our yard early that morning. Mom opened the door and we stepped outside to meet them. My heart felt like it was in my stomach. Mr. B. glanced over at me as the two ladies walked down the stone path. Suzanne was already stooping low with an outstretched hand to signal friendship with Mr. B. He came right to her without hesitation! He wisely knew we would never introduce him to anyone who wouldn't be kind to him. He accepted her immediately. He gently hopped right up to her as if he'd known her forever and she cuddled him in her arms. I then realized that Suzanne, like me, was a rabbit whisperer, because she talked very easily with Mr. B. As she held him close, her long dark hair flowed over his fur. I could hardly tell where Mr. B. ended and Suzanne began…they were like one beautiful being all melted together! It was clear right away that they spoke the same language of love.

After a few minutes, Suzanne placed Mr. B. back on the ground. She walked toward me as Mr. B. hopped next to her again and huddled close to her feet. He looked up at me with twinkling eyes that told me he was happy with Suzanne. He seemed contented beside her as though he'd always known her. She told us that her mother, Marianne, lived alone and had been ill for a long time. She spoke of how very much her mother loves animals…just like Suzanne does. She told us that Marianne had the perfect backyard for a bunny. It had a wooden fence that would give him plenty of room to hop, while keeping unfriendly animals out. She described the palm trees beside the fence that would shade him in summer and a covered patio that would protect his hutch from the rain. It sounded ideal…a better life for a bunny.

Suddenly, my mind became very quiet. I saw how beautiful Suzanne and Mr. B. were together and thought of Suzanne's mother, even though I hadn't met her. I imagined Marianne smiling as Mr. B. came into her life, just as I did the day he showed up here. Everything was pointing to his living in Los Angeles. It seemed that his life could be better there and he could make others happy, as well. Thoughts of keeping Mr. B. myself were already fading. Letting him move on was the right thing to do.

"But does your mom have any rose bushes?" I asked with sadness for his leaving.

"Many rose bushes," Suzanne sweetly replied.

"But will she talk with him, hold him, feed him treats and love him?" I asked with tears in my eyes.

"She will always do so," Suzanne said with a gaze of loving-kindness. Then she gently placed her arm around me. "And because I live near Mom, I will visit them most days to do the same."

"Well then," I found the courage to continue, "Mr. B. must go back to Los Angeles with you. It will save him from the cold weather and wild animals. And as much as I love him, I think your mother needs him more than me. I know he will help her feel better, because he's always done that for me. I know he would want to make life better for her." All at once, Suzanne and I stooped down to pick up Mr. B. together. We were thinking the same thing in that moment. We wanted him to know we both cared about him.

Mom, Mrs. Dennis, Suzanne and I talked a little more and we all agreed. Mr. B. would be safe, have lots of love around him, and be of comfort to Marianne. But giving up the friend I loved most in the whole wide world was going to be the hardest thing I'd ever done. Even so, I knew it had to be. Doing what would give happiness to others had become the most important thing to me.

Mr. B. was to make his journey south with Suzanne the very next day. We prepared his traveling box, complete with blanket, water and treats for his daylong road trip. His hutch was cleaned and placed in the back of the car so that it could shelter him again when he arrived at his new home. I kept a brave face so that nobody…especially Mr. B….would know how my heart ached to say goodbye. I placed a red rose on his blanket in the car. I wanted him to feel free to go.

Goodbyes almost always come too soon and that moment was here for us. We had a little time in our garden to talk before he was to make his trip. I sat down cross-legged and waited for him to hop beside me. He got one of those bunny smiles on his face as he came closer. In the blink of an eye, he gently jumped onto my lap. One of his long ears fell over my shoulder to give me a hug. I felt our hearts connect with love again as they had so many times before.

"Mr. B.," I said softly as I held him close, "You taught me so much about love that I never understood before. From you, I learned how to give more, care more and love another as I had only loved my own self. You taught me to think of others first. I'll miss you every day and it's very hard for me to let you go. But I must do so anyway. The best thing for you is to go home with Suzanne where you'll be safe, warm and loved. It's where you can do something truly wonderful for someone else. It's what you should do and where you should be."

Mr. B. looked up at me and his pink jewel eyes had turned crystal clear like *sparkling diamonds*! They were brighter than any light I've ever seen, but not blinding. I felt as though I was inside their brilliant glow. The light that surrounded us ran through every part of me. At that moment, I realized how very much I had inside me that I would give back to the world.

Then I heard Mr. B.'s comforting voice. I knew it would be a long time before I heard him speak again. "Michael, you've learned the meaning of true love. You actually knew it all along down deep inside. You fed me, sheltered me, and loved me, even before I showed friendship to you. That's called *unconditional love*. And I'll always be thankful for everything you gave me."

"But Michael, the kindest, most loving thing you've ever done is what you're doing today. Even though you wanted to keep me, you're going to say goodbye to me…and not just for my own good, but for someone else who needs me even more than you do…Marianne. You're exchanging your own happiness so that someone else can be happy. That's the gift of unselfish love and compassion. This is the kind of love that never ends. It's the reason that you will always be loved by others! You kept asking me why I was here. You now understand the reason. And where did I come from, Michael? *I came from a place in your very own heart*."

I felt a tingling all over as he spoke those words. It started at my heart and flowed upward and down…up to the tip of my head…down through my fingers and toes. It moved at the speed of thought…everywhere all at once! Everything that had happened started to make more sense. He'd come here to teach me that love is the real magic…and the more of it I give to everyone, the more I'll receive.

It seemed that the light from his eyes was shining right through me and everything else in the garden. It felt warm and never-ending. I was surrounded by the love I had given. It was as though he was me and I was him, and there was nothing dividing us. I breathed out and in. I closed my eyes and saved this sweet moment as a memory for the future. *He came from my heart and he'd always be there.*

We didn't have to say anything else. We understood each other completely. At that instant, I didn't feel sadness any more! The gift of love that had come to me wasn't really leaving me. In fact, it would never, ever leave me again, now that I understood where it came from and how to make it stay. By giving love to others, it would always come home to me. *The more I help others be happy, the happier I will be. Whatever I give comes right back to me*!

As Suzanne's car slowly drove away, I smiled and whispered, "Thank you, Mr. B., thank you, my friend." …and I'm sure he heard me, because I could see his eyes sparkling even brighter in my mind. I wanted him to know how much I'd learned from him. I wanted him to hear me say the words that my heart was speaking.

I watched as Suzanne and Mr. B. disappeared from view. Walking back into the kitchen, I was still happy from his words. I knew there would be special times to visit him. I knew this wasn't our last goodbye. It was just farewell for now and someday I would see him again. I took another deep breath, all the while feeling completely happy for the bunny and the people he was going to help. My sadness for his leaving had given way to joy for everyone. And I understood that even though I'd keep Mr. B. glowing in my heart as my most special friend, there was a whole universe of other beings out there who also needed my love.

Just then, I looked out the kitchen window. Some creature was stirring around in the garden. As I looked closer, she gazed up at me. The mysterious white cat, the one who always looks hungry, was sitting under a rose bush. Had she come to teach me something more? I opened the door to get a better understanding.

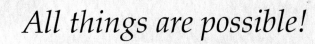

All things are possible!